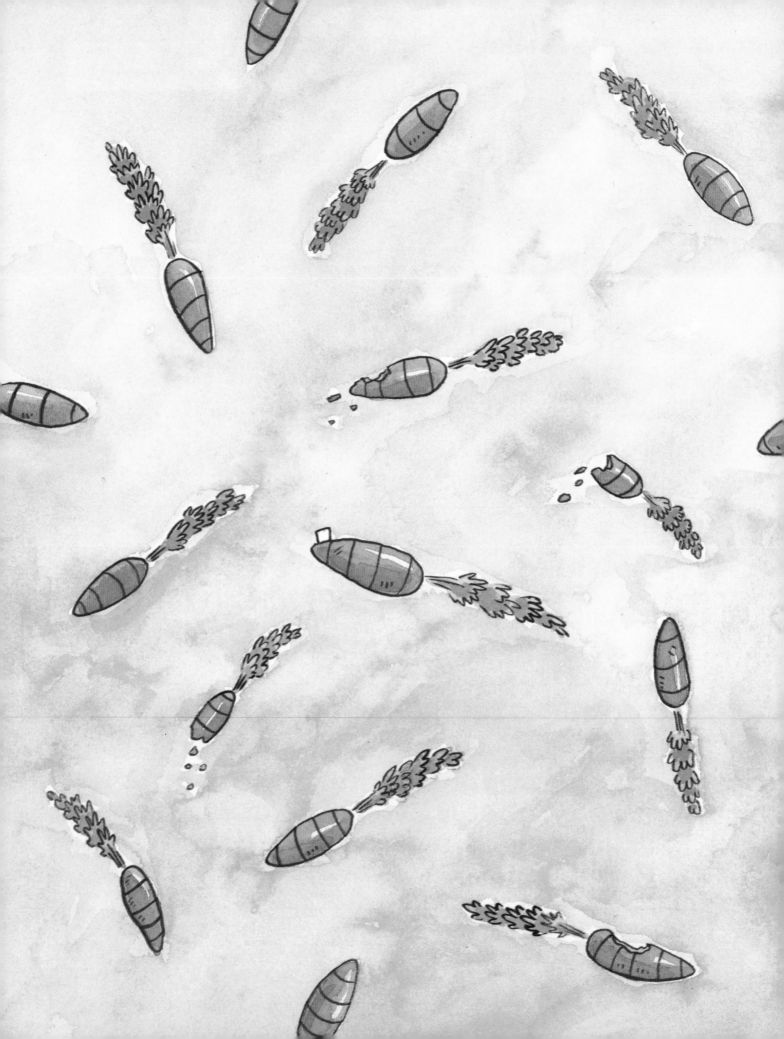

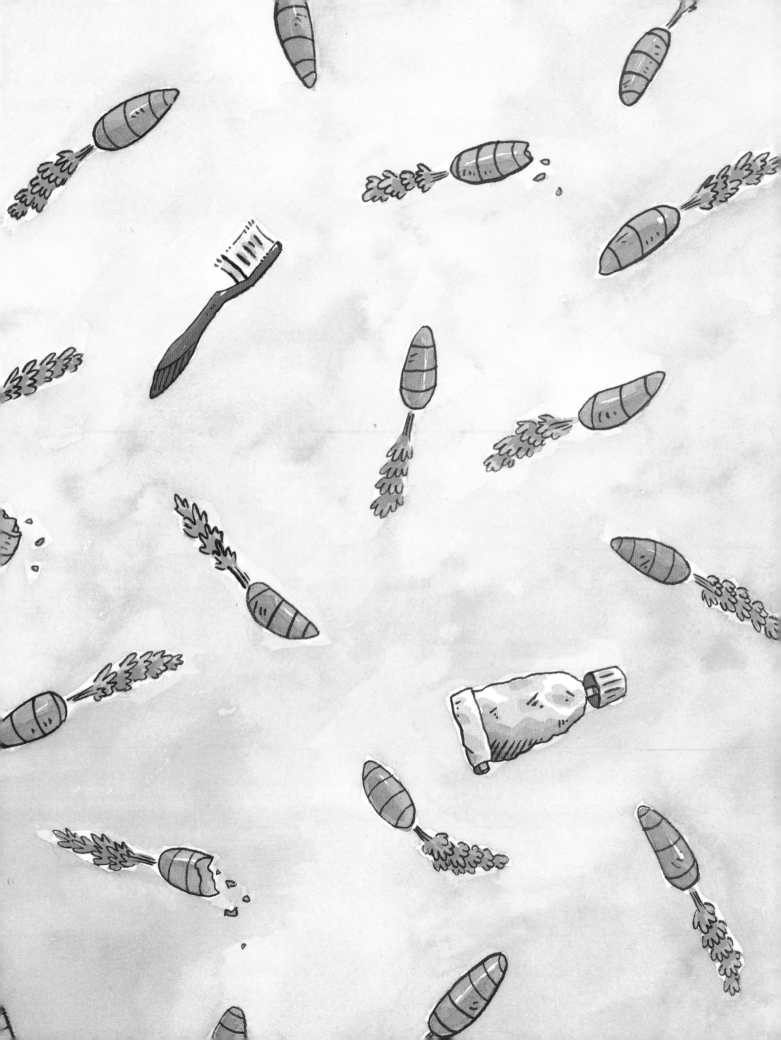

To our parents,
to Sara, Laura and Miguel

MYRIAD BOOKS LIMITED
35 Bishopsthorpe Road, London SE26 4PA

First published in 2004 by
MIJADE PUBLICATIONS
16-18, rue de l'Ouvrage
5000 Namur-Belgium

© Isabel Carralo, 2004
© Ronald Molitor, 2004
Translation Lisa Pritchard

ISBN 1 905606 22 2

Printed in China

Rainbow

Isabel Carralo
Ronald Molitor

MYRIAD BOOKS LIMITED

Rainbow Rabbit gets up early every morning. First she has a wash. Then she eats breakfast and watches the sun rise.

Rainbow's favourite food is carrots. Lovely, crunchy, juicy carrots. She grows them in her garden so she can eat a fresh one every morning for breakfast.

But today she's in for a BIG surprise…

She sinks her teeth into a lovely, crunchy, juicy carrot. Mmmmm…

But something doesn't feel right. Rainbow takes out the carrot and looks at it.

It's still a carrot… but now there's a tooth in it.

"That's strange," says Rainbow. "Carrots don't have teeth." Then she thought a bit more. "I've never seen a carrot with a tooth before."

Suddenly it dawns on her. "That's my tooth!" she wails.
"But I need it. I won't be able to eat carrots without it!"
"HELP! I want my tooth back!"

Rainbow stamps her foot. She's very angry. Just then her friend Heather Hedgehog comes up the hill.

"Whatever is the matter, Rainbow?"

"I've lost a tooth," Rainbow shouts. "And I need that tooth to eat my carrots." And she stamps her foot again.

"Goodness me!" says Heather.

Heather and Rainbow are just thinking what to do when something starts to flick earth at them. A little head pops out of the ground.

"Hellooooo," says Ted Mole. "Why are you making such a fuss? You woke me up."

Rainbow tells Ted all about her tooth. "Goodness me," says Ted. He thinks a little, and then he has an idea.

"I know, let's go and see the dentist. He looks after your teeth.
Maybe he can fix yours!"

"What's his name?" asks Rainbow.

Ted says, "I don't know. I've heard that he lives in the forest and has a bushy red tail."

"Will you both come with me to find him?" Rainbow asks Ted and Heather.

Who's that, perched on a rock?

"Excuse me, Mr Robin," says Rainbow. "Do you know where the dentist lives? He lives in the forest and he's got a bushy red tail."

"No, I've never heard of him.
But I can take you to the forest.
Follow me!"

Rainbow, Heather Hedgehog, Ted Mole and Mr Robin set off for the forest.

On the way they meet Philip Field Mouse. He's not very big but he has a long tail. He loves eating seeds and fruit and vegetables.

"No, I don't know where the dentist lives.
But can I come too?"

"Of course you can," they all say.

Rainbow, Heather Hedgehog, Ted Mole, Mr Robin and
Philip Field Mouse set off for the forest.

When they reach the first trees, they slow down.
It looks a bit dark and scary. Philip Field Mouse
sniffs the air. Who knows what they'll find in
the forest?

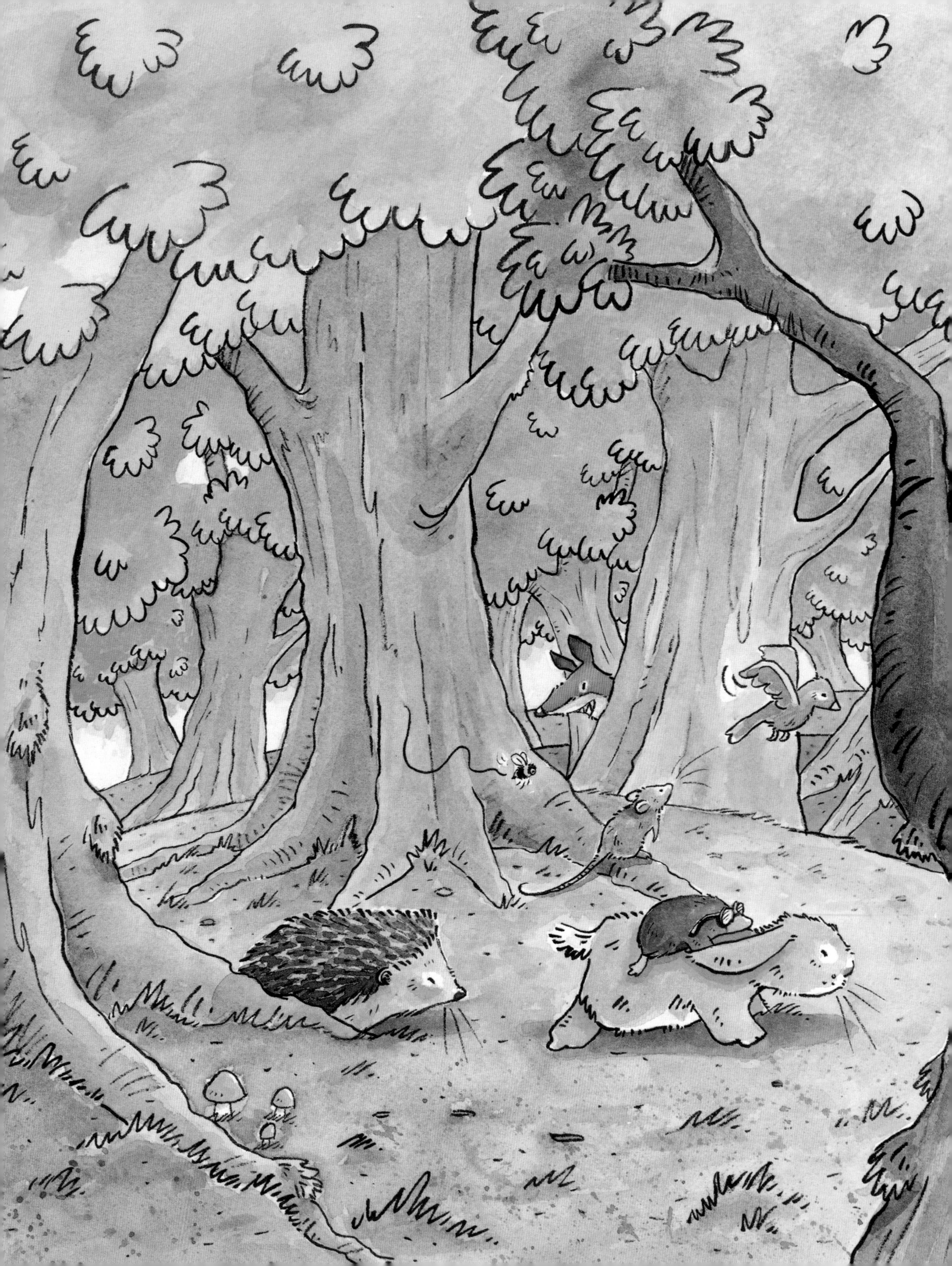

Philip Field Mouse gives a shout:
"Look over there! Can you see it? There's a bushy red tail!
It must be the dentist!"

Whose tail is that? Who lives
in the woods and has a bushy red tail?
He can run very fast and he's very
clever… but he's not a dentist.

That tail belongs to Mr Fox. He's not interested in
Rainbow's tooth. But he is hungry.

He thinks Rainbow will be a perfect meal, and then he will have
Heather Hedgehog, Ted Mole, Mr Robin and Philip Field Mouse for pudding.

Just as Mr Fox is getting close they all hear a voice.
"Quick! Come up this tree and you'll be safe!"

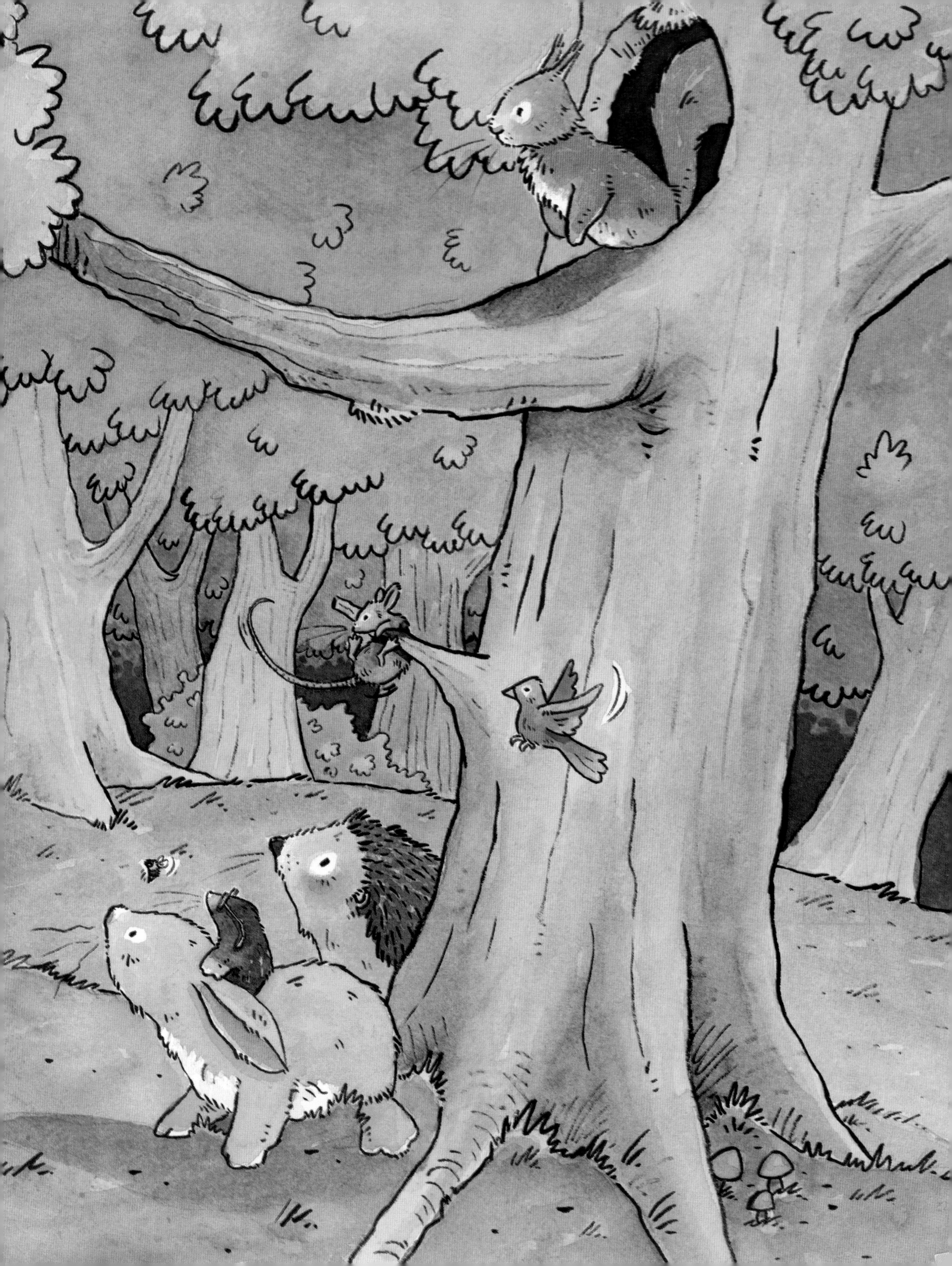

Quick as a flash the little animals
climb the tree.

(That's not easy if you're a
rabbit, or a mole or a hedgehog, but
when there's a fox chasing you, you do
your best!)

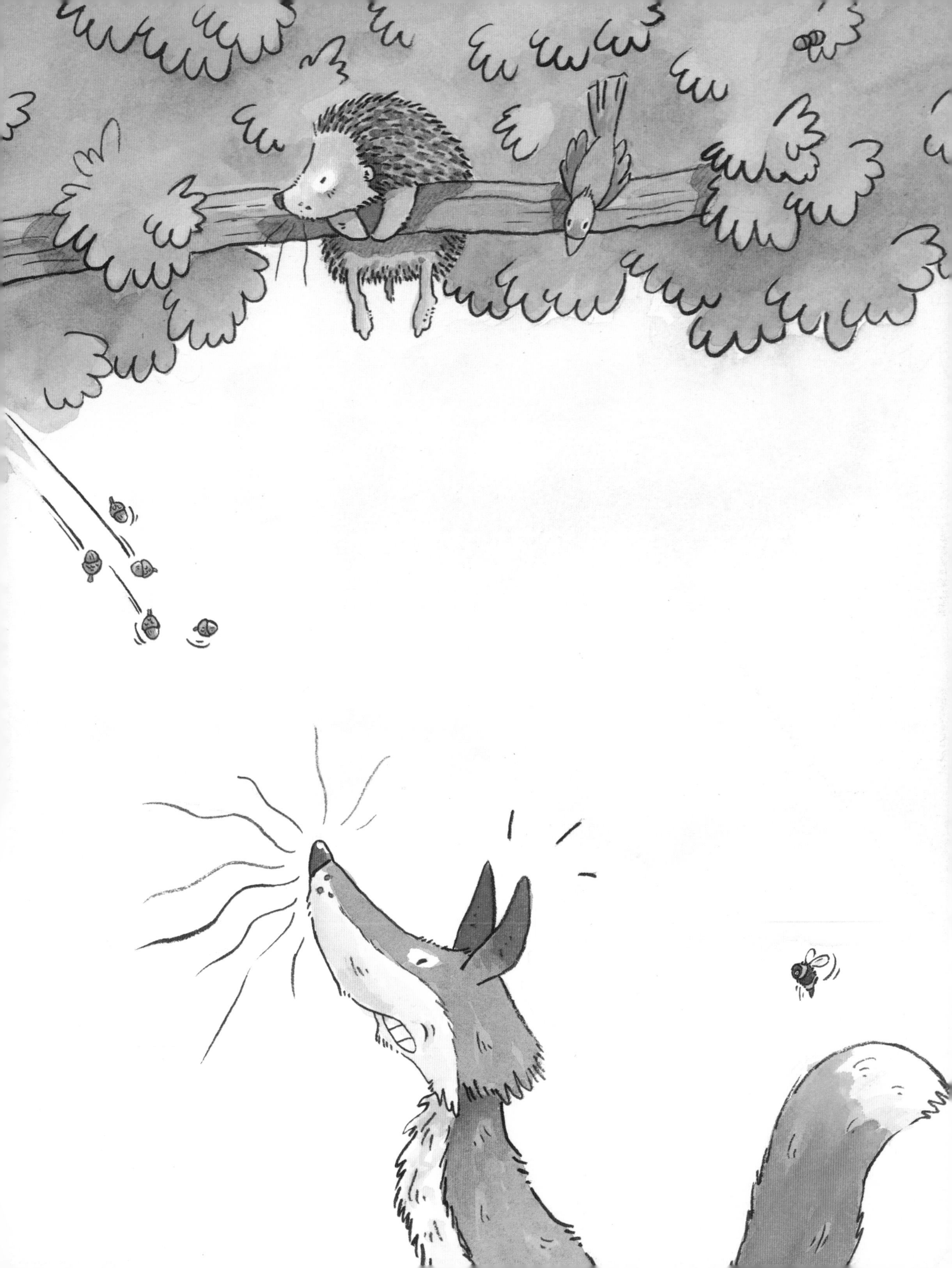

Mr Fox growls. Then he growls
some more. But Rainbow, Heather
Hedgehog, Ted Mole, Mr Robin
and Philip Field Mouse and their
new friend each take an acorn…
then they take aim…

And start to throw them at Mr Fox.
He runs off as fast as he can.
Rainbow, Heather Hedgehog, Ted
Mole, Mr Robin and Philip Field
Mouse all shout "Hurray!"

They turn round to their new friend.
Look! He has a bushy red tail.
"Well done everyone! I'm very glad to meet you.
My name is Sam Squirrel, and I'm a dentist. What
brings you to these woods?"

Ted Mole pipes up: "We came to see you. This is
Rainbow. She's lost a tooth and now she can't
crunch her carrots."

"Oh dear," said Sam the dentist. "Now then, Rainbow, open wide and let me take a look."

Rainbow opens her mouth. "Hmmm… There's nothing to worry about," Sam says. "Your gums are healthy and your new tooth is already starting to come through. It's all perfectly normal."

"Phew!" says Rainbow. "Thank goodness for that."

One by one the animals have their teeth checked. Sam takes
a good look. "Everyone looks fine!" says Sam.

When Mr Robin opens his beak,
Sam smiles. "You haven't got
any teeth to worry about, Mr Robin!
Birds don't have teeth."

Mr Robin feels a bit left out when everyone else gets
a new toothbrush from the dentist. When Sam notices
Mr Robin's sad face he holds a toothbrush out to him.
"Here's one for you too!"

Now everyone is happy with their visit to the dentist –
thank goodness they found Sam Squirrel with his bushy red tail!

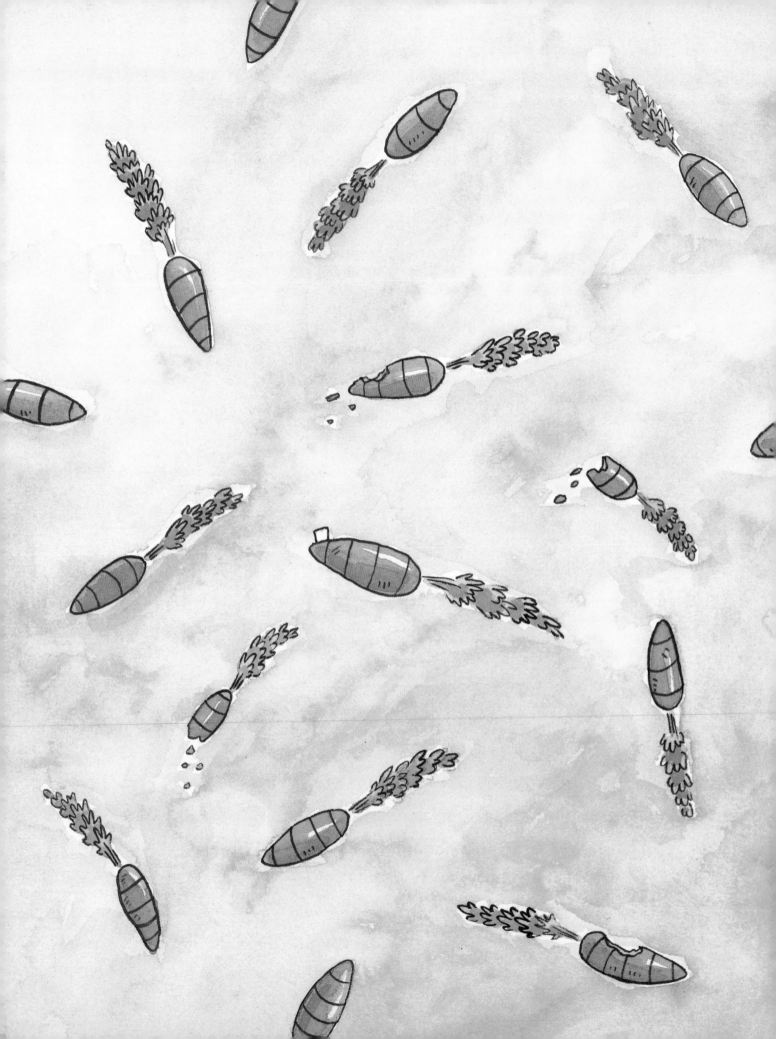

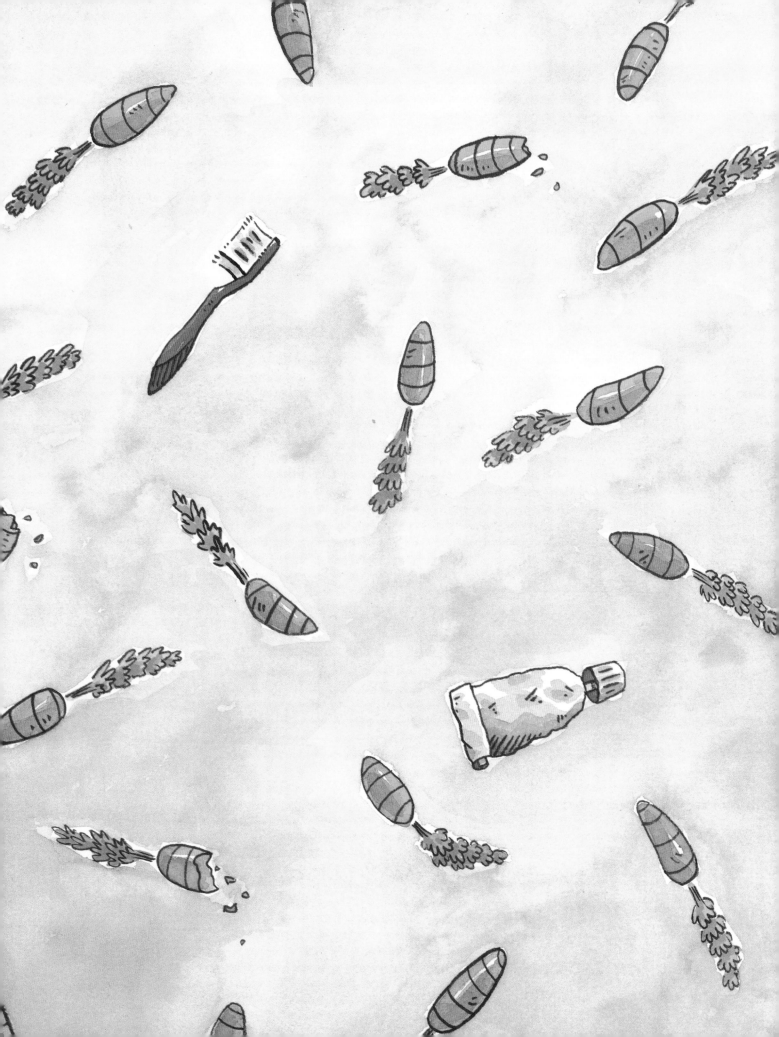